1 9 DEC 2017

Read more  books!

Meerkat Madness

More Meerkat Madness

Meerkat Madness: Flying High

Merry Meerkat Madness

Penguin Pandemonium

Penguin Pandemonium: The Rescue

Penguin Pandemonium: The Wild Beast

Panda Panic

Panda Panic: Running Wild

Raccoon Rampage

Raccoon Rampage: The Raid

Koala Calamity

Koala Calamity: Surfs Up

Otter Chaos

Llama Drama

Coming Soon:

Llama Drama: In It to Win It!

Penguin Pandemonium: Christmas Crackers

www.awesomeanimalsbooks.com

OTTER CHAOS!

Dam Busters

MICHAEL BROAD

Illustrated by Jim Field

HarperCollins *Children's Books*

First published in Great Britain by HarperCollins *Children's Books* in 2013
HarperCollins *Children's Books* is a division of HarperCollins *Publishers* Ltd,
77-85 Fulham Palace Road, Hammersmith, London, W6 8JB.

The HarperCollins website address is: www.harpercollins.co.uk

1

ISBN 978-0-00-748975-6

Printed and bound in England by Clays Ltd, St Ives plc

MIX
Paper from
responsible sources
FSC www.fsc.org **FSC** C007454

For Mama Broad

Woody

Sooty

Chip

Chapter One

The Curious Visitors

Woody Brown and Sooty Black darted along the riverbank, diving in and out of the water, and laughing as they raced each other home. The otter pups had spent the whole day chasing fish and skimming stones, but they were still full of energy.

"I wonder what our mums will be preparing for dinner?" asked Woody.

"Crayfish, I hope!" replied Sooty, drooling at the thought. "They're tricky to catch with those big snappy claws, but our dads fishing together usually grab enough for everyone, without getting a single nip."

The Brown family and the Black family lived together in a large old beaver lodge on the bank of the river. The two families had moved in as rivals and competed in the first-ever river races to decide who should stay, but they got on so well that they finally agreed to share. Pups, teens, parents and grandparents, eighteen otters in total, lived on a luxury island of twigs and branches called Cottonwood Lodge. With so many animals living under one roof, every mealtime was a big fishy banquet.

"Wait!" whispered Woody, stopping so suddenly Sooty almost crashed into him. The brown otter pup reared up on his hind legs and sniffed the air, twitching his whiskers.

"What is it?" whispered Sooty. He knew it had to be something important for his friend to stop so close to home, especially as it was almost dinnertime.

"I think someone was here a moment ago," said Woody, frowning and scanning the muddy ground. "But it wasn't an otter. Look at those strange tracks!"

He pointed to two long trails of flattened mud that led down to the water. It was as though whoever left them was dragging something flat and wide behind them, to cover their paw prints.

"Over there!" gasped Sooty, as he spotted two furry heads emerging from the river. The intruders were facing the other way, so the otter pups leapt into the bushes to hide and watch. The rust-coloured heads turned to reveal bulging cheeks and large front teeth that gleamed in the light of the setting sun.

"Beavers!" said Woody and Sooty together, peeping through the leaves as the strangers swam towards them. The beavers clambered up on to the bank and appeared to study the river. One was large with a huge flat tail and enormous yellow teeth, while the other was smaller and appeared to be the same age as the otter pups.

"Well?" said the big beaver gruffly. "Tell me what you think."

"I don't know, Papa," the young kit shrugged, awkwardly.

"Don't know?" grumbled his father, licking a claw and holding it up to the breeze. "What are your tingling teeth telling you?"

"Er, it's nice?" the youngster replied.

"*Nice?!*" the elder beaver exclaimed. He snatched a few leaves from the bush and tossed them in the river, watching their movement as they sailed downstream. He then surveyed the surrounding banks and high tree-line and took a deep breath.

"It's perfect!" he added gruffly. "Now come along, or your mother and sisters will be wondering where we are."

As the beavers dived back into the water and swam upstream, the two otter pups scrambled out of the bush, dusted off their glossy coats and frowned at each other.

"What do you think that was all about?" asked Sooty.

"I don't know," replied Woody. "But I think we should tell our parents about it when we get home."

Cottonwood Lodge was just round the river bend and when the pups arrived they hopped out of the water on to the mooring pad and scurried through the main entrance.

This led to a large central chamber with wide tunnels leading to smaller chambers, all bustling with otter activity.

Papa Brown and Papa Black had returned moments earlier and were busy dragging a basket filled with the day's catch to Mama Brown and Mama Black.

The Brown twins, Nutmeg and Chestnut, were playing tag with the Black twins, Storm and Shadow. They were darting in and out of every chamber, making as much noise as possible.

Coco Brown and Berry Black were in their room, which was an oasis of calm because the young female otters spent most of their time grooming and weaving flowers into jewellery.

In the central chamber Grandpa Jack
Black and Grandpa Bruno Brown were
telling tales of their youth as boxing
champions, while young surfer, Jet Black,
quizzed them on their many sporting
achievements. Grandma Maple
Brown was there too, but she
kept quiet as she didn't
like to encourage
the old otters,
even though she
was secretly proud
of her husband's
heavyweight boxing
titles. The younger pups,

Beanie Brown and Coal Black, were listening to the boxing stories too, while bobbing on their backs in the indoor pool and munching snacks from lily-pad plates.

All of the otters, Black and Brown, were busy having fun in their own unique ways, living in happy otter chaos at Cottonwood Lodge. But every one of them stopped what they were doing when they heard the fishing basket open; all were eagerly waiting to see what was for dinner. Mama Brown and Mama Black slowly squinted inside the basket, nodded in approval and cuddled their husbands. Papa Brown and Papa Black then tipped the contents out on to the floor for everyone to see.

"HOORAY!" cheered the otters as a massive haul of crayfish poured out.

Woody and Sooty were so excited at the sight of their favourite meal that they forgot all about the beavers they had seen. It was only after dinner, when everyone had eaten their fill and a little bit more, that the youngsters remembered their strange encounter.

"We saw beavers today," said Woody, sucking on a crayfish claw.

"Where?" asked Grandpa Bruno, narrowing his eyes.

"They were round the bend in the river," replied Sooty.

"How many?" asked Grandpa Jack, sitting up straight.

"Two," Woody and Sooty replied together.

They were surprised that their grandpas had shown such interest in the beaver sighting. The old otters usually fell asleep after dinner, and sometimes during. Papa Brown and Papa Black sat up too and frowned at Mama Brown and Mama Black. Then they all shook their heads and chuckled their secret fears away.

"Two beavers don't mean anything," said Papa Brown.

"This used to be a beaver lodge, after all," added Papa Black, indicating their fine surroundings. "So we should expect one or two beavers passing through here from time to time."

"They mentioned a mother too," said Woody.

"And sisters," added Sooty.

"A whole family?" said Mama Brown, furrowing her brow.

"Oh, I'm sure it's nothing to worry about," chirped Mama Black, seeing the frowning young otters peering up at her. And when the other adults saw the concerned looks on the youngsters' faces, they immediately agreed and smiled.

"There's nothing to worry about," said Papa Brown.

"Nothing at all," added Papa Black.

"It's getting late," said Mama Brown.

"Time for bed then," said Mama Black.

"Yes, come along, sleepy pups," said Grandma Maple merrily, herding the young otters towards the indoor pool. "Let's get those paws and furry faces washed and then it's off to beddie-byes for all of us!"

Woody and Sooty thought the beaver sighting was odd, but hadn't really thought there was anything to worry about. Not until their parents started saying there was nothing to worry about!

"Why do you think everyone behaved so strangely when we mentioned the beavers?" whispered Woody, as they lay in their grass and moss beds.

"Maybe they think the beaver family are the ones who used to live here," said Sooty. "And they're afraid they might want to take Cottonwood Lodge back."

"But the beavers didn't come this far down river," said Woody. "And they would know where their old home was. It looked to me as though they'd never been around these parts before."

"I agree," said Sooty, with obvious relief. "So there's probably nothing to worry about after all. The grown-ups are just being weird again, as usual."

Woody and Sooty both laughed until a series of loud "SHHH!" noises came from the other chambers. They stifled their giggles and settled down to sleep, happy in the knowledge that all was well in their riverside world and nothing terrible was going to happen.

Chapter Two

Waking the Beast

The following morning was warm and sunny, but instead of waking to the sound of birds singing cheerfully and dragonflies fluttering dreamily, the two otter families were startled awake by the familiar voice of Beanie Brown, from outside the den.

"SOMETHING TERRIBLE HAS HAPPENED!" she cried.

There was a sudden surge of activity as dozens of panicking otters raced out of their chambers, through the tunnels and out on to the mooring pad, where they found Beanie gazing into the tranquil water.

"What's wrong, my darling?" gasped Mama Brown.

"Yes, tell us, my dear," added Grandma Maple.

Woody Brown knew his shy sister could become even more unconfident when put on the spot, so he stepped alongside Beanie and held her paw. "What is it?" he whispered.

Beanie frowned at Woody and then pointed to the water.

The assembled otters moved closer to the edge of the mooring pad and peered into the river, expecting to see something terrifying like a crocodile or an alligator. What they saw was… absolutely nothing.

"There's nothing there, sis," whispered Woody.

"I know," said Beanie, sniffing and wiping her shiny black nose with a paw.

Woody Brown looked into the river again and considered why Beanie might be up before everyone else and what could possibly make her scream in terror – and then gasped when he eventually worked it out.

"The fish have all gone!" he said.

"Fish don't just vanish overnight," said Grandma Maple, dipping her tail in the water and swishing it from side to side, in the hope of drawing a few nibbles to the surface. "They must be just hiding."

As the main providers of food for both families, Papa Brown and Papa Black dived into the river. They darted about deep underwater, stirring up clouds of bubbles intended to scare up any fish that might

be lurking at the bottom, but there was nothing except riverweed, rocks and old empty shells.

Mama Brown clutched the paws of Mama Black as their husbands returned to the surface and shook their heads gravely. The rest of the otters appeared baffled by the mystery, with the exception of Grandpa Bruno, whose eyes widened as he understood what had happened.

"Beavers!" growled the old otter.

"Beavers!" agreed Grandpa Jack.

"How could beavers steal all of our fish?" asked Woody.

"They don't *steal* them," said Grandpa Bruno. "They *stop* them."

The old brown otter jumped into the water and swam to the middle of the river where he could see past the bend. "They've built a dam right across, just a short way upstream," he yelled. "All of our fish have carried on swimming downstream and no new ones can get through."

"They've blocked the flow of the river!" gasped Grandma Maple.

The black and brown otters all dived into the water and swam out to Grandpa Bruno and saw for themselves that the dam was huge. There was an enormous felled tree, its trunk stripped, stretching from one bank to the other. Along its length the trunk was piled high with branches and logs, all packed tightly together with mud and grass. There was also the bristly roof of a lodge on the riverbank that had to be the beavers' home.

"Everyone back to Cottonwood Lodge," growled Grandpa Bruno, snorting through his nostrils. "I'm going to have a polite word with our new neighbours."

"I'll come too," added Grandpa Jack. The old black otter knew only too well how hot-headed Bruno could be and wanted to keep an eye on him.

"You're not going without us!" said Papa Black and Papa Brown.

"Be careful, all of you," warned Grandma Maple, looking fretful. "I don't want any trouble."

Mama Black and Mama Brown made their husbands promise to be safe and to look after the old boxers, whose advancing years had done nothing to quell their fighting spirit. Then the two wives hugged and rubbed noses with their husbands, waved them off and herded the young otters back to the lodge.

Along the way the mother otters answered questions about beavers from Coal and Beanie, calmed fears of fish-oil

shortages from Coco and Berry and told the two sets of twins to stop squabbling, all the while assuring Grandma Maple that Grandpa Bruno would return in one piece. So it was no wonder they failed to notice that two young pups were missing.

Woody and Sooty had crept away to spy on the elder males, swimming silently as they approached the dam. Then they hid behind an overhanging tree and watched as Papa Black and Papa Brown called into the entrance of the beaver lodge. The grandpas were grumbling and growling like a pair of grumpy gargoyles.

"Hello?" called Papa Black.

"Is there anyone home?" added Papa Brown.

"They must be home," said Grandpa Jack.

"Eating our fish, no doubt!" snorted Grandpa Bruno.

"Stop that," warned Papa Brown. "We're being polite, remember?"

Papa Black was about to call into the dark hole once again when he heard movement from inside. The four otters stepped back just as a big rust-coloured beaver stepped out, bleary-eyed and scratching his head.

"What's all this noise about?" he growled, and then yawned. The beaver had obviously been fast asleep and didn't appreciate being woken up. "Don't you know I work nights?"

"Well, that's what we've come about," said Papa Black, motioning to the felled tree and mesh of branches blocking the flow of water. "You appear to have spent the whole night building a dam that happens to be very close to our lodge."

"Our river level is now rather low and moves much more slowly," added Papa Brown, seeing how high the river was on the other side of the dam. "And it also appears to be entirely fish free."

"So?" said the beaver.

"We were wondering if you wouldn't

mind moving it somewhere else," Papa
Black smiled, hopefully. "You see, there
are eighteen otters already living on this
section of river, all with hearty appetites,
and *we* were here first."

There was a long silence during which the frowning beaver seemed to consider the otter's suggestion to move. He looked at the four adult otters in front of him; he looked at the two young otters hiding behind an overhanging tree branch, and then he looked up at his dam.

"No," said the beaver, and made his way back inside the den.

"Ooh, let me at 'im!" growled Grandpa Bruno, already swinging his paws, but Grandpa Jack held him back until the moment passed.

Suddenly, the beaver reappeared, followed by five other beavers.

"This is my wife, Twiggy," he said, motioning to the eldest female, who had obviously heard everything and was scowling at the otter intruders. "And those are my daughters, Holly, Willow and Hazel – also known as the Saw Sisters."

"The sore what?" asked Papa Brown.

"The Saw Sisters," the beaver repeated proudly. "They can fell a tree in thirty seconds and have won prizes for bark-stripping, stick-stacking and branch-breaking. You name it – they've won prizes for it."

The three grown-up daughters ground their huge teeth menacingly.

"My name is Chuck," the beaver concluded, and folded his arms defiantly. "And after we spent the whole night building a brand-new dam and cosy lodge to live in, *we're not going anywhere!*"

"You forgot one!" yelled Woody from behind the rustling branch.

It was then that the head beaver frowned and remembered the youngest member of his family. The kit was standing behind his sisters, scratching in the muddy ground with a stick.

"Oh," said Chuck with obvious disappointment. "That's Chip."

The young kit lifted his head at the mention of his name and smiled at the adult otters. Then he saw the otter pups behind the tree and waved at them.

"Chip was meant to be a chip off the old block and take over my dam-building business," growled Chuck, clearly comfortable sharing his parental sorrows with perfect strangers. "But all he does is

scratch around in the mud."

"He does his best," sighed Twiggy, patting Chip's head.

"Hmmm," grumbled Chuck.

"Now look here!" growled Papa Brown, thinking that the head beaver was trying to get his own way by changing the subject. "We were here first, so according to river rules that means—"

"Don't you live in Grinder Grime's old place?" interrupted Chuck.

"Well, we didn't know his name, but it *was* an abandoned beaver lodge," said Papa Brown. "That's not the point, though. Cottonwood Lodge is *our* home now and—"

"Beavers were here first, then," said Chuck, thumping the muddy ground with his wide, flat tail. "So maybe it's the otters who should move instead!"

"I'll show you who needs to move, and I'll even give you a hand!" growled Grandpa Bruno, swinging his right hook before Grandpa Jack could hold him back.

Twiggy and the Saw Sisters joined Chuck and started thumping their tails in steady, war-like drumbeats that were obviously intended to warn off attackers. And it appeared to work. Having promised their wives to stay out of trouble and look after the old boxers, Papa Brown and

Papa Black exchanged a few mumbles and retreated, tugging Grandpa Jack and Grandpa Bruno away with them before they charged the dam.

The beavers looked very pleased with themselves as they bundled back inside the lodge. All except Chip, who paused to prod the dam with his stick, frowned at it, and then followed his family inside.

Woody and Sooty left their overhanging branch and hurried after their elders, who were swimming back downstream. Their fathers were up front, with their grandpas close behind still grumbling about honour and bravery and wanting to give Chuck the beaver a knuckle sandwich. The two young pups trailed behind everyone, looking and feeling completely deflated.

"I can't believe our dads backed down," said Woody.

"I think the beavers are very selfish," retorted Sooty.

"Shellfish!" gasped Woody. "No more clams and mussels!"

"And no more crayfish," gasped Sooty. "No more fish at all!"

"I don't think we'll be able to stay here if there're no fish," sighed Woody. "And I like living together. It's so much more fun than when our families lived in separate dens."

"You don't think we'll have to split up, do you?" asked Sooty.

"I don't know," said Woody. "But I doubt there are many other dens that two families would fit in so comfortably."

The young pups looked ahead at their

fathers, who they thought must be feeling pretty awful after their confrontation with the beavers ended so badly. Just then Papa Black and Papa Brown looked back and caught the looks on Sooty and Woody's faces.

"Cheer up, otters!" smiled Papa Black, with a twinkle in his eye.

"Last one home's a bubbly fish fart!" smiled Papa Brown.

Both otters winked at their pups before diving down with a splash. They soared underwater at high speed, taking the lead as they raced everyone home. The grandpas, always keen to show how fit they still were, also joined the race.

"Our dads seem strangely cheerful," frowned Sooty.

"That must mean they've got a plan!" exclaimed Woody, and the two friends shared a happy high-five, before diving underwater with a double splash and zooming after the others.

Chapter Three

The Plan

"All otters gather in the central chamber!" yelled Papa Brown, leaping out of the river and on to the mooring pad, with Papa Black following close behind. The rest of the returning group clambered after them and hurried into Cottonwood Lodge.

When everyone was assembled, Papa Brown called for quiet and then addressed the two families. Sooty and Woody sat at the back and couldn't wait to hear their fathers' plan of action.

"Our meeting with the new neighbours did not go well," said Papa Brown gravely. "In fact, it went very badly indeed. The beavers refuse to move their dam and we don't know what to do about it."

The otters all gasped and stared, wide-eyed, at him.

"However..." prompted Mama Brown, elbowing her husband.

"Huh?" said Papa Brown, who was always

bad at giving speeches.

"The good news is that we all have different skills and talents!" Mama Brown continued, opening her arms wide. "And if we all put our furry heads together, we're sure to come up with something brilliant!"

"HOORAY!" cheered the otters.

Papa Black stepped forward and began to scratch on the mud wall with a stick.

"There are six beavers in total," he said, drawing six beaver-shaped blobs in a line and in order of size. "And the dam stretches the entire width of the river, blocking the flow of fish to us," he added, drawing a wiggly line with a bend in the middle and two thicker lines cutting across the top.

"Where are we?" asked Nutmeg, raising her paw.

"Don't you know where you are?" chuckled Chestnut, mocking his twin sister as usual. "Nutmeg doesn't know where she is!"

"I meant in the diagram, nitwit," Nutmeg groaned.

"We are right about *here*," said Papa Black, following the river bend with his stick and drawing a cross to mark the location of Cottonwood Lodge. "And the water flows in *this* direction, from *here* to *here*," he added, drawing a curved arrow from the dam to the lodge.

"Now we just need to find a way to make

these go away," said Papa Brown, pointing at the pictures of the beavers. "Or to make *this* go away," he said, pointing to the dam.

"Turn the beavers into toads!" giggled Storm.

"Or turnips!" giggled Shadow.

"Turnip toads!" they giggled together.

"Thank you for your input," sighed Papa Black, shaking his head and casting his eyes over the sea of black and brown fur. "Does anyone have any non-magical solutions?"

"Can't we ask them nicely to go away?" whispered Beanie.

"I'm afraid we've already tried that, my darling," smiled Mama Brown. "Though, I suspect if the female otters and female beavers got together, we might still arrive at a sensible solution."

"Hear, hear!" said Mama Black.

"You didn't see the female beavers!" said Grandpa Jack. "I think they were more into chomping than chatting. What did they call the three daughters?"

"The Saw Sisters," said Papa Brown. "They were pretty scary."

"Well, I think we should set a pack of wolves after them!" growled Grandpa Bruno. "The only danger there would be making sure we didn't get eaten ourselves."

"That's a little extreme, even for you," frowned Grandma Maple. "Having beavers in our back yard is bad enough; we don't want wolves at the door as well."

Papa Brown was beginning to look rather worried. "Does anyone have any other suggestions at all? What about Coco and Berry?"

"We can't concentrate with those two

whispering!" growled Coco, pointing an accusing finger at her little brother and his friend at the back of the chamber. "Otherwise we probably would have come up with something really, really clever."

"Woody and Sooty," said Papa Black. "Do you have any thoughts you'd like to share?"

"Holes!" said Woody, jumping up excitedly.

"Excuse me?" said Papa Brown.

"We can make lots of little holes in the dam," said Sooty, also jumping up and down. "That way the beavers can stay where they are, but the fish can carry on swimming down the river as usual."

"And the beavers probably won't even notice," added Woody.

"Holes…" pondered Papa Brown, scratching his chin. "I like it!"

Papa Black turned back to the wall and started prodding the drawing of the dam with the end of his stick, making little holes all along its length. He then added lines showing water flowing through and drew baffled expressions on the blobby beavers' faces.

"Holes!" he said cheerfully.

"Holes!" confirmed Papa Brown.

"HOLES!" cheered the otters.

"All we need now is a crack team of dam busters and a cool name for the operation," said Papa Brown, obviously excited to be taking action at last. "Any suggestions?"

Storm and Shadow swiftly put their paws up.

"Any suggestions that don't involve toads or turnips?" added Papa Brown, at which the twins lowered their paws with a sigh. "A name that will inspire greatness in the brave team entrusted with this mighty task?"

There were cries of "Woodworm Warriors!" and "Operation Fish Holes!" and "Beaver Deceivers!" Then Woody put his paw up and waved at his dad. "You've already given it a name!"

"What did I say?" asked Papa Brown.

"Dam Busters!" said Woody. *"Operation Dam Buster!"*

The otters selected for Operation Dam Buster were not the most obvious choices, but they were the ones most likely to work quickly and quietly and with the least amount of fuss. So Papa Brown and Papa Black left Cottonwood Lodge with Woody and Sooty because they had come up with the idea of Operation Dam Buster in the first place – and were far more responsible than their older brothers and sisters. The beavers would still be sleeping in their lodge and they needed to stay that way for the plan to succeed.

"I wish we could just be friends with the beavers," whispered Sooty as the young pups turned the bend in the river and followed their fathers towards the dam, swimming slowly with their heads just above the surface of the water.

"Me too," agreed Woody. "There's enough fish for all of us."

"Our dads did *try* to talk to them," said Sooty, "but they didn't seem very friendly at all."

"Maybe it's because we woke them up?" said Woody. "I know Grandpa Bruno can be grumpy when he's disturbed. Grandma Maple tells us all to hush when he's having a nap so as not to wake the ogre!"

The four otters reached the dam and Papa Brown and Papa Black made paw signals to instruct Woody and Sooty to dive underwater and spread out along the length of the structure. When the dam busters were in position they began to pull away lumps of grass and moss and removed some of the smaller branches, letting them rise to the surface and drift downstream.

The two adults continued to give paw signals through the murky water, and the pups dashed up and down the dam, seeking likely locations for brand-new holes. Despite wishing to make friends with their new neighbours, the young otters were having a brilliant time pulling apart the beavers' enormous dam. In fact, they were having so much fun they got a little carried away.

"I've made seven," said Woody as they came up for air.

"I've made four," said Sooty. "But they're all bigger than yours."

"Not for long!" laughed Woody, diving back under as his friend chased after him.

They had both started out making small holes, but when they discovered that only small fish could swim through, they made the holes wider to let the large fish through, for bigger meals.

Papa Brown and Papa Black were no better with their hole control, so when the dam busting was finished there were more holes than dam and white water was gushing through in torrents. All that remained of the structure was a mess of loose logs and branches clinging to the central tree trunk. Soon the whole thing began to bend and creak as the full force of the river pounded against it. Eventually there was an enormous crack that sent the otters rocketing to the surface.

The tree trunk splintered in two under the pressure of the water. The thinner top end drifted downriver, along with the remaining logs and branches. The thicker root end remained anchored to the bank, supporting the bristly mess that was the beaver lodge. The otters bobbed up and down in the water and drifted downriver with the broken dam. They clambered on to the treetop to rest, riding it home like a giant canoe.

"I think the beavers might notice that," frowned Woody.

"I think you're right," replied Sooty.

"Well, maybe it will teach them a lesson – not to mess with otters and their fishy food supply," said Papa Black, patting the pups' heads. "They started it by building the dam in the first place."

"I doubt we'll have any more trouble from the beavers," said Papa Brown. "Not now they know who they're up against. I imagine they'll simply pack their stuff and move on, as we originally suggested."

The otters ate a modest mussel dinner served with daring tales from Operation Dam Buster and, having solved the beaver problem once and for all, everyone was in high spirits.

"We dashed about like lightning," said Woody, whooshing his arms about to show how fast they moved, "making holes in that huge dam and watching shoals of fish dart through!"

"But we stayed completely silent," whispered Sooty, "because we could hear those mean beavers snoring their heads off while we worked under their very noses!"

"WOW!" gasped the rest of the young otters, gripped by the story.

"But that's not the best bit," said Woody, nudging his friend.

"Then we broke the whole thing wide open!" added Sooty excitedly.

"BOOM!" roared the pups, jumping up with their paws in the air.

Everyone chuckled and clapped with delight, happy that the otters had triumphed against the beavers. They were also keen to fill their rumbling bellies with fishy goodness.

The otters all went to bed early that evening so they could rise early the next day and reap the rewards of Operation Dam Buster. After a night of regular water flow the fish stocks would return to normal and by morning the river would be jam-packed with delicious food.

Chapter Four

Chomping and Chasing

The following day the otters got up bright and early and dashed out to the mooring pad. One by one they dived into the river to catch their own favourite fish for a celebratory breakfast banquet.

"I bet I catch the biggest fish!" boasted Woody.

"You wish!" replied Sooty.

Woody and Sooty then back-flipped into the river, with a cry of "CRAYFISH!"

Coco and Berry stayed on the mooring pad and planned to point at the fish they wanted, but then Jet did a somersault over their heads and splashed into the water, soaking them through. The females shrieked and jumped in after him, swiftly followed by all of the other hungry otters.

Everyone was in a great mood until they realised that something was missing. It certainly wasn't otters because every member of the Brown and Black families was present… it was the *fish* that hadn't turned up!

The otters scoured every centimetre of their section of river but couldn't find a single clam or crayfish. They eventually gathered in the middle, treading water and looking around. It was then that they turned their heads upriver, past the bend, and saw a sight that made their empty mouths drop open.

"They can't have!" gasped Papa Brown.

"But how?" gasped Papa Black.

The otters swam upriver to find an even bigger dam than the one they had destroyed. It was a monstrous mound of tree trunks, logs and branches that loomed over their heads and cast everyone in shadow.

"You have to give them points for effort," sighed Mama Brown.

"They must have been at it all night long!" said Mama Black in amazement.

The otters spread out along the colossal structure, looking for any cracks or weak points, but the wood was solid and any gaps had been tightly packed with grass and mud.

"This one's not going anywhere," frowned Grandpa Black, patting the wood.

"I could probably punch through it with a few good swings," bragged Grandpa Bruno, air-boxing as he bobbed up and down in the water. "It's a good job the beavers are hiding or that big one would finally get what's coming to him!"

"I imagine they're sleeping like pups after all this work," said Grandma Maple.

"WRONG!" roared a voice from above.

The otters looked up and saw the head beaver, Chuck, appear at the top of the dam. His wife, Twiggy, swiftly followed, scowling at the intruders. Then the Saw Sisters appeared, looking even more ferocious than before. The beavers all gnashed their teeth and snarled like wolves. They looked pretty terrifying, towering over the otters, until Chuck glanced left and right, rolled his eyes and sighed.

"CHIP!" he growled through the corner of his mouth. His hind paw tapped impatiently as the young kit clambered up the dam, fell backwards into the water, and then clambered back up again.

"Grrr!" Chip croaked, rather weakly. He wobbled back and forth as he struggled to stay upright on the uneven platform of branches.

His father turned back to the otters.

"You destroyed our dam!" he said gruffly.

"Technically, yes," confessed Papa Black, smiling awkwardly. "But it was more of an accident, really..."

"It's actually quite a funny story involving holes," chuckled Papa Brown. "You'll probably laugh when you hear it."

The head beaver snorted through his nostrils and looked as though he'd never laughed once in his whole life, and wasn't about to start now.

"The time for talking is over," said his wife, nodding to the rest of the family, who all cracked their knuckles and bared their teeth. "Now it's time to start chomping!"

The beavers leapt off the dam together

76

and belly-flopped into the river, causing six huge splashes that poured over the startled otters. Beanie squealed at the top of her voice and everyone else looked around in a panic.

"Swim for your lives!" yelled Mama Brown, taking Beanie's paw.

The otters dived underwater with eighteen rapid tail-splashes and then fanned out. The dam limited their escape options so they headed for home at speed.

The beavers took off after them, zigzagging back and forth, their teeth chomping like turbo-powered wood-chippers, but the otters were faster in the water owing to their long sleek bodies and narrow tails. They also didn't want to have their bottoms bitten. The beavers might be less agile swimmers, but they had strength and sharp teeth, and their flat tails worked like fins, propelling them through the water like furry piranhas.

When the otters turned the bend in the river, they all sprinted for the safety of Cottonwood Lodge. The beavers were only chasing the adults, really, so the young otters reached the lodge first. They leapt out of the water on to the mooring

pad, swiftly followed by the grown-ups. Once they'd all scrambled inside, the Blacks and the Browns collapsed in a wet heap, gasping for breath.

"Are they still out there?" panted Mama Black.

"What are they doing?" gasped Mama Brown.

The papas and grandpas peered though the holes in the woven outer walls of the lodge and scanned the river. Chuck and Twiggy were bobbing in the water, glaring at the otter lodge. They shook their fists when they saw otter eyeballs peeping at them.

"Stay away from our dam!" yelled Chuck.

"Or we'll smash this place to splinters!" added Twiggy.

The pair flicked their tails crossly before paddling back upstream, followed by their three large beaver daughters. Chip, however, was only just arriving. His sisters shook their heads and motioned for him to turn round and head back to the dam.

"They're going home now," said Grandpa Jack.

"Good riddance too!" growled Grandpa Bruno.

"We're lucky they didn't attack the lodge," said Papa Black, patting the sturdy wooden structure. "With their teeth they could have turned it into a pile of sawdust in no time."

"Especially after what we did to their dam," agreed Papa Brown. "I know it was an accident and we only wanted to make a few holes, but they must think we set out to demolish it."

"They're builders," said Grandma Maple wisely.

"What do you mean?" asked Mama Black.

"Maybe it's not in their nature to destroy things," she explained.

"They destroy trees," said Mama Black.

"And cut off other animals' food supplies," added Mama Brown.

"Perhaps they didn't mean to cut off the fish," said Grandma Maple. "Maybe it was just an accident and we've misjudged them."

"If that's true then we may still be able to reason with them and reach a compromise," Mama Brown said hopefully. "When the dust has settled, of course."

"They might even let a few of us climb the dam each day to fish on the high side of the river," said Mama Black. "Or dig an underwater access tunnel."

"I'm not crawling through a dam!" gasped Coco. "It snagged my coat just swimming near it earlier. I'd probably go bald if I had to crawl through a hole with twigs pulling out tufts of fur!"

"I agree," huffed Berry. "I'd rather eat riverweed!"

"Maybe we should all eat riverweed," said Grandma Maple, fully aware that plans made in the heat of the moment were not always the best. "At least until everyone calms down – us and the beavers. Then we can all come back together and decide what to do."

"We should fight to the death!" snarled Grandpa Bruno.

"Hear, hear!" growled Grandpa Jack.

"I think you've both done enough fighting for one lifetime," Grandma Maple replied firmly. "Now we're going to try

the *opposite* of fighting and see where that takes us."

"What's the opposite of fighting?" the old otters said together, frowning.

"Eating vegetables!" she smiled.

Chapter Five

The Wild West

The following days of eating only vegetables did not have the calming effect on the otters that Grandma Maple had hoped for. Mama Black and Mama Brown sent everyone out to forage for any interesting edible vegetation they could lay their paws on and everyone came back with riverweed. There were a couple of berries and a few tufts of grass too, but the rest was riverweed – great slimy mounds of the stuff!

Mama Black and Mama Brown then set to work preparing a selection of new meals. On day one there was riverweed soup, which was riverweed served in river water. Day two was riverweed stew, which was riverweed in river water, with extra big lumps of riverweed. Day three saw a special riverweed salad, with a grass and berry garnish. But a bird swooped down and grabbed the berries, so it became just a pile of riverweed with grass on it. On the fourth day they prepared a vegetarian version of their ever-popular fish wraps. These certainly looked the part, but where the original recipe called for delicious oily fish-heads to be dunked in clam juice and then wrapped in riverweed, all that was inside the new version was more riverweed.

No one took to being vegetarian and everyone became increasingly bad tempered, all secretly wondering if their bellies would ever feel full again.

Woody and Sooty sneaked out one night and returned to the overhanging tree, just to gaze at the moonlit dam and imagine all the crayfish swimming on the other side.

"Think of all those crunchy claws!" sighed Woody.

"And the tasty tails too," added Sooty.

"Hello!" said an unfamiliar voice behind them.

The otters squeaked when they saw a beaver bobbing in the water, its big teeth gleaming in the moonlight. Then they realised it was the young kit, Chip, and he was smiling at them cheerfully.

"Hello," the otters replied together.

"I'm sorry about the dam and the fish," Chip said awkwardly. "And for chasing your family down the river. My dad is pretty stubborn when it comes to his building work."

"It's not your fault," said Woody. "And we did break the last dam."

"Our parents can be just as stubborn," added Sooty. "Grown-ups are weird."

"Do you want to play?" Chip asked hopefully. "I've been working on an obstacle course that I usually run on my own, but it'll be much more fun with three of us!"

The otter pups nodded eagerly and followed the beaver up the bank as he vanished into the woods. Chip led the otters to a huge adventure playground he had built himself, using logs and vines and anything else he could lay his paws on. There were rope-swings, seesaws, slides and climbing walls, all running up and down and round the trees.

"WOW!" exclaimed Woody and Sooty.

"Last one round is a rotten clam!" laughed Chip.

The beaver ran for the start line, with the otters chasing after him and catching up in no time. The otters were faster, but the beaver was familiar with the obstacles, so the trio overtook each other throughout the whole course, tugging tails and roaring with laughter. Woody and Sooty then helped Chip build even more obstacles from plans he scratched out in the mud. The otters and the beaver raced each other a few more times until they all collapsed

in a heap, rolling around and giggling, like the very best of friends.

"I thought your dad said you were no good at building," panted Woody, looking up at all the complicated network of ramps and pulleys. "What you've done here is completely brilliant!"

"You should definitely show this to your

dad," added Sooty. "Once he sees how clever you are, he'll be bragging about you like he does about your sisters chopping down trees."

"I've tried to make my dad look at my plans and ideas, but he thinks they're silly and won't work," sighed Chip. "He only ever wants to build traditional dams, and I prefer coming up with designs for new ones."

"Well, we like your ideas," said the otters.

When they got up the next morning, Woody and Sooty noticed that their families were much grumpier than the day before. Even Mama Brown and Mama Black had lost the will to invent new dishes and simply sculpted the riverweed into fish-shaped blobs for breakfast.

To take their minds off their own rumbling bellies, Woody and Sooty made a secret game out of watching all the members of their families to see who would crack first. They both expected Grandpa Jack or Grandpa Bruno to be the first, seeing as they were pretty crabby to begin with and had spent the whole week moaning. Or Nutmeg, who had taken to wearing a clamshell on her nose because a side effect of only eating riverweed was gassiness. All the otters had been farting non-stop, including Nutmeg herself!

Coco and Berry were pretty fed up too when they ran out of fish oil and their fur began to frizz. They looked like a pair of over-pampered poodles. But, as it turned out, the one who eventually snapped was the least vocal otter of them all.

"I CAN'T TAKE IT ANY MORE!" shrieked Beanie, startling everyone with her sudden outburst. As the otter who loved food the most, she was the one

who had been the most miserable, but she spoke for all of the otters when she sobbed, "I MISS MY FISHY FOOO-OOO-OOD!" at the top of her voice.

"That's it!" said Papa Brown, standing up heroically and casting aside the soggy remains of his fish-shaped riverweed blob. "I'm going out fishing for crayfish. I may be some time!"

This would normally have been the point where the otters lifted their spirits and cheered, "Hooray!" but they simply frowned at each other and then looked at Papa Brown strangely.

"There are no crayfish, dear," said Mama Brown, standing up and patting her husband's head, wondering if the riverweed had finally addled his brain. "The fishes have all gone away, remember?"

"There are none in *this* part of the river," sighed Papa Brown, "but there's a stream a short way west of here where I can lay my paws on all the crayfish we can eat."

"The Wild West!" gasped Mama Brown, swooning at the thought.

"It's not as bad as all that," replied Papa Brown.

"Anywhere away from the safety of the river is too dangerous!" said Mama Black, fanning her friend. "The Wild West is mostly forest, and we all know otters can't always make a fast getaway on land."

"We've been there before," said Papa Black, standing alongside his hunting partner. "If we're cautious and watchful it will be perfectly safe. We'll be back before you know it with a huge crayfish feast!"

Mama Brown looked at the other otters and sighed. Beanie was wiping her tears away and had already started drooling at the mention of crayfish. The rest of the black and brown otters were all gazing at Mama Brown hopefully.

"Well, if you're sure it's safe," she relented, giving Papa Brown a big hug – and taking the opportunity to whisper a word of warning. "But if you get eaten by a bear, I will never speak to you again!"

"Can I come?" asked Woody, jumping up and down excitedly.

"Me too!" said Sooty.

"Not this time, my darlings," said Grandma Maple, patting the young pups' heads. "Your dads will need their wits about them in the forest, and I'm going to need an extra pair of volunteers to prepare for the feast."

"Awww," sighed Woody and Sooty, who knew when they were being given the brush-off.

"We need to go alone the first time, to make sure there's no danger," said Papa Brown. "But once we know our way around the forest, there's no reason why we shouldn't take you on the next outing. It's almost time for us to start teaching you to forage for yourselves."

"Hooray!" cheered Woody and Sooty together.

Fortunately, Papa Brown and Papa Black returned from the Wild West later that day, laden with fresh crayfish and salmon. The fishing expedition had been a complete success and they encountered nothing more dangerous than a low-flying butterfly.

The feast that followed was full of family cheer and everyone was happy to have their diet, and their lives, back to normal.

The following day Papa Brown and Papa Black went out west again, but this time with Woody and Sooty, who paused every few moments to look, sniff and listen for danger. It was their first time out foraging in the forest and the pups' enthusiasm was matched only by their excitement.

"Now, always stay close," said Papa Brown, as the otters dashed from one tree to the next, sneaking through the forest like furry ninjas. "And never spend too long out in the open, or in any high place where you might be spotted."

"How do we find the stream?" asked Woody.

"Look for clouds of tiny insects, and pay attention to where birds and dragonflies are flying to," said Papa Brown, pointing overhead at a speckled thrush that was swooping in and out of the overhead branches, flying in the same direction they were heading. The thirsty thrush was swiftly followed by a pair of tiny warblers. "The birds always know where the water is because they are high up and have a good view."

"But always remember that other animals will want to use the stream and are watching too," warned Papa Black, pointing in the distance to where a lone wolf was wandering away in the opposite direction. "Not everyone is friendly, so you need to be aware of who's about."

"This is such a brilliant adventure!" Woody said to Sooty.

"I know!" agreed Sooty. "Remind me to thank the beavers for stealing our fish. Without them we might never have been allowed to explore the Wild West!"

The otter dads let the pups take the lead for the rest of the way. Sooty and Woody looked around the forest for clues to take them to the water, using all the new skills they had learnt, just like a treasure hunt.

When the otters finally arrived at the stream they all leapt in to the water, darting and diving about, searching for fish to catch. Between the four of them, working together as a team, they managed to haul a feast of fishy goodness that would last both otter families for several days.

Everyone was in high spirits on the way home, laden with fresh fish and not a single strand of riverweed. They laughed about how huge the crayfish were and how much fun it had been to chase them down; how the salmon leapt out of the water, so they had to catch them in the air, and how they found oysters hiding among the rocks. The otters were over halfway home when Papa Black suddenly froze and hushed the others.

He stood tall on his hind legs and sniffed the air, whiskers twitching.

SNIFF

Sooty was about to do the same, thinking this might be another training exercise on how to keep a look-out for danger in the forest, when his dad screeched at the top of his voice, dropped the haul of fish and nudged the pup forward with his nose.

"RUN!" yelled Papa Black, and the pair raced away.

Woody didn't have time to wonder what was going on before Papa Brown did the same to him, and he immediately remembered what to do. The first lesson he and Sooty had been taught, before they even entered the forest, was to head for the river as fast as you can when the alarm is given, and not to look back.

Woody and Sooty sprinted more quickly than they ever had before. They darted between trees, under bushes and over fallen branches. The young otters were fast, but nowhere near as fast as their dads, who ran just behind them, never overtaking but zigzagging from side to side with incredible speed.

The pups could hear the footfalls of a much larger animal bearing down on them. The beast was puffing and panting as it tried to catch their nimble fathers, who were dashing about like deer. The chase caused such a ruckus that it startled birds in the trees, who cawed and flapped away.

Somehow the pups remembered the way back through the forest. Not only that, but they had the good sense to take the shortest route to a different section of the river, as they didn't want to lead the pursuer to their home. This meant heading south until they reached the curved section of river between Cottonwood Lodge and the beavers' dam. Woody and Sooty burst through the trees and soared over the muddy riverbank. They plunged straight into the water with two big splashes, and two even bigger splashes immediately followed, as their fathers dived in too. The older otters motioned for the pups to keep swimming underwater, all the way to the bottom of the river.

There the otters sat on the murky riverbed and gazed up at the sunlit surface. Papa Black and Papa Brown pointed as the silhouette of an enormous head appeared.

It was a mountain lion! The p

at the beast with wide eyes an

cheeks. They almost gasped w

but knew to hold their breath. Th

only young, and not yet an ex

hunter, but he had enormous

claws and seemed like a giant

to them. The otters watched an

trembling in the predator's shado

Chapter Six

A Temporary Truce

The mountain lion sniffed the air and looked about, then dipped his mouth into the water and took a few laps before turning on his tail and padding slowly back into the forest. Moments later the otters swam quickly to the surface, gasping for breath. Once they were sure the big cat had gone, Papa Brown and Papa Black led the pups home.

Woody and Sooty felt a little shaken, but they were mostly thrilled to have had such a close encounter with a dangerous animal and couldn't wait to brag about it to the others. But the impact of their bragging was somewhat ruined by the cuddles and kisses from Mama Brown and Mama Black.

"You are *never* to go to that stream again," said Mama Black, hugging Sooty so hard that he squeaked. "It's much too risky with a lion prowling the forest."

"The same goes for you," agreed Mama Brown, licking her paw and flattening the

ruffled fur on Woody's head. "We can all live without crayfish."

"But—" started Grandpa Bruno, who was promptly silenced by a look from Grandma Maple.

Later that day the otters left the safety of the lodge to forage for more food and the elders insisted that they all stay close together. There was a chance that the mountain lion could try its luck again, now it knew there were otters this side of the river.

"Everyone keep an eye on the riverbanks," said Papa Brown, who led the trail of hungry otters across the river, like a mother duck followed by her ducklings. "Any sign of movement and you screech at the top of your voice and dive under."

The youngsters did as they were told, but seemed more excited than frightened by the danger.

"That mountain lion is lucky I wasn't there," Chestnut said to Woody, throwing air-punches like his grandpa. "I would have bopped him on the nose and sent him yelping back into the forest."

"Yeah, right," scoffed Nutmeg. "I would have been much braver than you."

"I would have jumped on the big cat's back and ridden him through the forest," said Jet, grooming his Mohawk fur-do. "You two are so lucky to get close to a real mountain lion!"

"It was pretty scary," said Sooty, enjoying the attention.

"His paws and claws were *huge*," said Woody, flexing his own paws and spreading his claws wide. "Not to mention his teeth. I think he could have gobbled us all up in one go!"

"He was so fast!" said Chip. "I'm glad you got away!"

The otters were startled by the voice and looked around to see the young beaver kit behind them. They were so surprised at his sudden appearance that they nearly gave the alarm screech.

"You saw it too?" asked Woody, swimming over to his friend.

"We came up over the dam just as you all dived in," said Chip. "The mountain lion was right behind you!"

"We could hear his paws on the ground!" said Sooty, swimming over to join them.

"And his loud breathing," added Woody, doing an impression of a panting lion

with his tongue hanging out, which made everyone laugh very loudly.

The rest of the otters swam over to hear what Chip had to say about the predator. The kit appeared to be out in the river alone, so they made sure not to crowd around and frighten him.

"Has your family seen him since?" Grandma Maple asked kindly.

"Yes, ma'am," Chip replied shyly. "We've seen him stalking at the edge of the forest. Dad says to keep a constant lookout and stay close to the river."

Just then Chip's dad rose out of the water, followed by Twiggy and their three daughters. Chuck looked as bad-tempered as ever. He motioned for his son to join his sisters, who all tutted with disapproval as Chip approached them. Twiggy's mood didn't seem any better and she nudged her husband to say something to the otters.

"We wouldn't need to look out for mountain lions if you lot hadn't led one to the river where we live!" growled Chuck, picking at his huge front teeth with a fish bone.

"Well, *we* wouldn't have been chased by a mountain lion if you hadn't built that stupid dam," growled Papa Brown, waving a paw at the enormous wall of wood.

"How do you work that out?" scoffed Chuck.

"We only happened upon the mountain lion because you stole all our fish and forced us into the Wild West!" retorted Papa Black. "It was the only other place we could get a decent meal to feed our families."

There was silence for a moment, broken only by snorting and snuffling from both camps, and much puffing out of chests as the situation turned into a stand-off between the otters and the beavers. Grandpa Bruno swung his paws, while Grandpa Jack held him back.

"No one is entirely to blame," Mama Brown said firmly.

"Well, if you ask me—" said Twiggy.

"If we asked you," interrupted Mama Black, smiling hopefully at the beaver, "I'm sure you would agree that no good can come from our husbands fighting. Especially when we have young ones to protect against a common enemy."

Twiggy screwed up her nose and frowned as she thought about what had just been said to her. Then she looked at Chuck and her children and nodded in agreement.

"So I propose that we put all our differences aside for now and join forces," added Mama Brown, smiling at the beavers. "And I would like to invite you all back to Cottonwood Lodge, where we can tackle the problem of the mountain lion… together."

Chapter Seven

An Unexpected Plan

The otters and beavers somehow managed to cram into the central chamber at Cottonwood Lodge. Papa Brown and Papa Black stood before the mud wall that they had previously used as a drawing board.

"I would first like to offer a very warm welcome to the beaver family!" said Papa Brown, smiling at the beavers. "And I'd like to welcome all the otters back to what has become our secret mission headquarters. It seems like only yesterday we were in here plotting to get rid of those pesky—"

"Eagles!" interrupted Papa Black.

"Eagles?" frowned Papa Brown, and then realised what he'd been about to say. The purpose of their last big meeting had been to get rid of the beavers and their dam. "Yes, eagles!" he added quickly. "Horrible things – flapping about with their sharp talons."

"What eagles?" said Chuck. "I haven't

seen any eagles."

"That's because we shooed them all away," said Papa Black, turning to the wall and using his stick to draw a weird blob shape. "But now we are up against this chap here!" he said, pointing to the picture.

"A crocodile?" said Twiggy, tilting her head.

"No," said Papa Black. "A mountain lion."

"That looks more like a crocodile to me," said Twiggy, glancing around to see what everyone else thought of the drawing. "It definitely doesn't look like a lion."

"It does have a reptile quality to it," agreed Chuck.

Papa Black sighed and quickly shortened the tail and added some whiskers. He looked back to Chuck and Twiggy, who squinted at the drawing and shrugged.

"Anyway... this mountain lion has come after us once and now he's lurking at the edge of the forest," said Papa Brown. "Big cats like him are partial to an otter or a beaver for lunch, so it's only a matter of time before he tries again. We need to find a way to stop him coming back here for good."

"Otters and beavers both have their own unique skills, and with so many of us we should be able to come up with a plan," added Papa Black. "Now, does anyone have any ideas?"

The young otters offered the usual suggestions, ranging from trying to speak to the mountain lion nicely, pushing him off a cliff, or turning him into a toad or a turnip. The eager otters all put something forward, but nothing was heard from the beavers.

"Do any of the beavers have any ideas as to how to get rid of the mountain lion?" asked Papa Brown, casting his eyes across the sea of black and brown heads, and resting on three rusty red ones grouped in the middle.

The Saw Sisters stared back at him and said nothing. Had they been asked to chop down a tree, or chomp through a log, they would have been first in line, but coming up with ideas wasn't really their thing. Neither was talking.

Twiggy saw her daughters looking uncomfortable and quickly spoke up. "The crocodile could scare the mountain lion off," she said.

"Or the eagles," said Chuck. "It's a shame you got rid of them."

There was an awkward silence during which the otters all looked round, wondering whether the beavers were joking or if crocodiles and eagles were the best they could come up with.

"We beavers are builders," Chuck growled angrily, standing up and waving his arms about. "Well, most of us are. Chip has yet to fell a tree or stack a log and is a huge disappointment, but the rest of us *build*!"

"We know what you do! It's your building that got us into this mess in the first place!" said Papa Brown bitterly, who would not be yelled at in his own lodge. "What's your point?"

"I'm saying, if you come up with a plan that relies on good, honest building, then we'll build it for you," said Chuck, sitting down again defiantly. "But I have yet to hear a single suggestion that isn't full of holes, and if there's one thing beavers hate, it's holes!"

The adult otters agreed with the beavers that none of the proposals would work on their own. They were about to suggest that everyone take a break when they noticed Woody and Sooty waving at the back of the chamber.

"Chip has a plan!" said Woody.

"And it's a really clever one," added Sooty.

"Oh, this should be good," Chuck grumbled sarcastically. The Saw Sisters narrowed their eyes at their brother, but a look from their mum told them to be quiet until they'd heard what he had to say.

The young beaver kit made his way to the front and swallowed.

Chip had been happy to plot and plan with his otter friends, who both thought his ideas were brilliant, but when it came to explaining them to the grown-ups, he suddenly became shy. Woody and Sooty quickly joined him at the front of the chamber and revealed the whole plan while the beaver kit took the stick from Papa Black and turned to the mud wall behind him.

Chip wiped out the drawing of the peculiar crocodile-mountain-lion mutant and then drew a grid across the wall. He proceeded to map out his plan as the otter pups described each phase in great detail. The beaver also made a little drawing of each contraption to be built and indicated the size it needed to be.

The Saw Sisters watched the plan unfold and although they didn't completely understand it, they were still impressed that their little brother, who was rubbish at building, had a talent for inventing

things that *others* could build. Twiggy was
beaming at her son's hidden genius, and
kept nudging Chuck. But her husband
was not a beaver who would change his

mind easily. Chuck had only ever wanted a son who could build a dam, so that he could follow in his paw prints. He simply watched and grunted from time to time until his son stopped drawing and the otter pups stopped talking.

"Well?" said Papa Brown excitedly, stepping up to the front again and addressing the scowling Chuck, the smiling Twiggy and the befuddled Saw Sisters. "Can you build it?"

"Of course we can build it," said the head beaver, scratching his chin as he scanned the complicated blueprint, while Chip stood next to it and hoped to see a flicker of pride from his father.

"But whether it will work or not is another matter entirely!"

Chapter Eight

To Catch a Mountain Lion!

The beavers worked through most of the night to get the various elements of the contraption built and set up round the site of Cottonwood Lodge. Chip had given up trying to impress his dad, but was determined to see his plan succeed.

He oversaw all of the building work and instructed the beavers to make minor modifications as they tried and tested each part of the apparatus. The otters

also stayed up most of the night, working out their part in the plan, which was very dangerous. It needed several rehearsals, with the help of the beavers, and by morning everyone was ready to put Chip's grand plan into action.

Papa Brown and Papa Black bounced up and down on the mooring pad, preparing for the task ahead. Their role was to head back into the Wild West forest and lure the mountain lion to the river. It was a perilous mission, but vital for the plan to work, so their wives were each trying to put on a brave face.

"Now make sure you don't get caught," said Mama Brown, hugging Papa Brown before the two of them rubbed noses. "You'll be no use to any of us in the belly of a mountain lion."

"Promise me that you'll keep a safe distance," said Mama Black, hugging Papa Black tightly.

"I promise," gasped Papa Black. "We'll both be fine."

"And we'll be looking out for each other," said Papa Brown.

"Are you sure you don't need backup?" asked Woody.

"We've outrun him before!" Sooty added eagerly.

"That's very brave of you both," said Papa Brown.

"But someone has to stay behind and look after everyone else," whispered Papa Black. The two pups nodded in agreement and hugged their dads.

Mama Black and Mama Brown clutched each other's paws as they watched their husbands clamber up the steep bank. They reached the tree-line, waved back at the onlookers and then disappeared into the forest.

Papa Brown and Papa Black had been putting on a brave face too, because neither of them wanted to meet the mountain lion again. But their families were counting on them, so they took a deep breath, wished each other the best of luck and dashed between the trees. The two otters looked and listened and sniffed with every step, using all of their senses to find the beast before it found them – and it didn't take very long at all.

"There!" whispered Papa Brown, pointing to a flicker of movement in the distance. The otters hid behind a tree and watched, and sure enough the mountain lion stalked into the clearing. It was almost as though he was waiting for the otters to return.

"It's now or never," said Papa Black. "Are you ready to run?"

Papa Brown took a deep breath and nodded, then the pair hopped out from their hiding place and began to laugh and

play noisily, pretending they had no idea the big cat was there, and when he turned in their direction they acted as though he had taken them by surprise.

"Oh, what rotten luck!" said Papa Brown, speaking at the top of his voice for the benefit of the beast. "It's that big, scary mountain lion we escaped from yesterday!"

"I expect we're in trouble now!" added Papa Black, putting his paws up to his open mouth. "I hope he doesn't come after us again as we run home to all the other yummy otters and delicious beavers!"

The otters paused for a moment and watched the mountain lion take it all in, just to make sure he'd take the bait and give chase. For a moment he frowned at them, trying to work out why they were acting so strangely. Then he lifted his head and roared, before bounding after the otters with all his might.

"Off we go, then!" chirped Papa Brown, turning tail, along with Papa Black. "And let's hope that little beaver, Chip, knows what he's talking about!"

They raced back the way they had come, bounding through the undergrowth, moving like black and brown bolts of lightning. When they reached the edge of the forest, they gave a signal to the others, waiting on the riverbank below, to indicate that the big cat was on his way. Everyone took their positions, just as Papa Black and Papa Brown dived off the edge of the slope and hit the top of the mudslide on their bellies.

The mudslide was at the back of Cottonwood Lodge. It zigzagged down the bank, before ending in a steep wooden ramp at the water's edge. The mountain lion had no idea the slide was there, so when he leapt after the fleeing otters he landed on his bottom and skidded after them at high speed.

Papa Brown and Papa Black zoomed expertly down the mudslide and hit the ramp at the same time, soaring through the air and diving into the water. But, just before the lion reached the ramp, Woody and Sooty sprang out of hiding and went to work, pulling a heavy wooden lever that dropped a catapult cup in its place. The creature's world turned upside down and, before he knew what had happened, he slid into the cup and spun like a top.

It took a few seconds for the big cat to stop spinning, and when he did he was sitting in front of the brave pups, who waved goodbye as they pulled another lever that launched him back into the air again.

"YEEAAAW!" screeched the mountain lion, flying towards the river.

Cats – even the giant variety with massive paws – don't like water. So, after a big splash, he quickly bounded back up the bank and on to a sloping deck made from rows of smooth logs. But, the moment he set a paw on the deck, the logs spun round and, no matter how fast he ran, he stayed on the same spot, like training on a treadmill.

"Bring on the rain of pain!" yelled Twiggy, standing on a rock.

Out in the river the young otters, Chestnut, Nutmeg, Storm, Shadow and Jet, were poised next to floating baskets filled with twigs and small stones. At the beaver's signal they began to toss handfuls of debris through the air and, using her tail as a bat, Twiggy hurled them inland at the mountain lion.

"YEAW! YEAW! YEAW!" he yelled as the mini missiles rained down.

THWACK!

HUD

The sticks and stones were only small and bounced off the startled cat as he struggled on the spinning logs. Before long, though, some of the stones got lodged in the gaps, jamming the contraption long enough for him to leap off. The lion hit land, turned and snarled angrily. He sniffed and searched for any otters or beavers close by. Twiggy had already vanished and the young otter pups were safe in the water. The only one out in the open now was Grandma Maple!

"Oh, please have mercy, Mister Mountain Lion," she sighed, clasping her paws together as she stood quivering beside a bush, a little way up the bank. "I am but a poor, elderly otter."

The big cat growled menacingly and charged at Grandma Maple, not realising that her paws were clasped round another wooden leaver. This lever released another catapult, which showered the ground between them with broken clamshells.

"YEAW! YEAW! YEAW!" yelled the mountain lion again as he landed on the sharp shells, springing up and down like a cat on a hot tin roof.

Grandma Maple made a speedy getaway and was swiftly replaced by Mama Brown and Mama Black, who eyed the animal up and down with fierce disapproval.

"If you leave now that'll be an end to it," said Mama Brown.

"But you must *never* come back here again," added Mama Black.

The mountain lion stopped springing, planted his paws on the sharp shells with a defiant wince and glared at the otters. Mountain lions don't speak the same language as river mammals, although most animals can make themselves understood if they speak slowly and wave their paws about. The big cat understood the offer and responded by leaping towards them with a deafening roar.

Mama Brown and Mama Black expected as much and hurried away, leading the pursuer up the bank to where Coco and Berry were waiting. By this point in time, the mountain lion had grown wise to the tricky otters, and looked about before approaching them, checking for levers and shells or things they might throw at him. But there was nothing except a strong smell of fish lingering in the air, so he made his way up the rocky slope towards the two grinning otters... and then abruptly slid straight down again as the pups released a glossy stream of fish oil. Coco and Berry waved their greasy paws at him and then slicked back their fur triumphantly.

The mountain lion scrambled frantically, trying his best to stop the downward slide, but he was entirely at the mercy of gravity. He slipped further towards the final contraption in the otters' and beavers' plan. Chip was there to pull the lever.

Before the lion knew what was happening, a large wooden cage scooped him up and suspended him on the high end of a huge seesaw plank – the other end of which was weighted down with rocks.

"YEEAAAW!" the lion bellowed angrily.

"HOORAY!" cheered the otters as they

swam to shore, or hurried out from their
hiding places on the riverbank. The beavers
could see the plan had been a success, but
they were not yet relaxed enough to rejoice
with their neighbours.

"You did it!" yelled Woody and Sooty, and immediately dashed over to Chip. The otter pups heaved the beaver kit up on their shoulders and did a lap of honour, plonking him down right in front of his dad.

Chuck looked at his son and, being a beaver of very few words, he simply smiled and patted him on the shoulder. Chip had seen him do this with his sisters, usually after they'd finished building a new dam together, so he knew it was an enormous display of pride.

"You're a chip off the old block after all," said Chuck, gazing up at the trapped lion. "You may not have the skills of a builder, but you obviously inherited my brains."

"I'll remind you of that next time you get your teeth stuck in a tree trunk and I have to pull you out by your tail!" laughed Twiggy. Then she gave Chip a big hug and added, "You are smarter than both of your silly parents put together. We never should have doubted you."

Chip's sisters joined the family hug and the otters gathered round, smiling.

"It's not quite over yet," warned Papa Brown, stepping up to the cage and frowning at its snarling contents. The mountain lion was suspended in the air and safely out of reach, but this didn't stop the big cat from swiping his paws through the wooden bars.

"Now we have to negotiate with him," added Papa Black, joining his friend as he cleared his throat, to try to reason with the lion.

"As you can see, we are very good at defending our borders," stated Papa Brown, in a calm and level tone. "But we would like to offer you a truce so that we may all live here in peace, without fear."

The lion gave a rumbling growl and narrowed his huge eyes.

"We will set you free and let you leave here unharmed," Papa Black continued, taking over from his friend. "But you must *never* return to this part of the river again."

"Do we have an understanding?" asked Papa Brown.

The mountain lion scowled, but appeared to consider the offer, then he made his answer known by swiping his talon-like claws at his captors and yowling angrily. He bounced up and down in the cage and the otters and beavers took a big step back as the seesaw began to creak under his weight. The mountain lion obviously noticed that too because he stopped and grinned, and then gripped the bars with his paws and began to bounce even harder.

"This is not how it was supposed to go," said Chip, scratching his head as the mechanism groaned and wobbled. "He was meant to admit defeat and slink back into the forest!"

"I'm not sure that seesaw will hold out much longer!" added Chuck, watching the plank flex and splinters begin to form in the middle. "In fact, now might be a good time to—"

Before the beaver could finish what he

was saying, the wood split in two with an enormous crack and the cage came crashing to the ground. The drop broke enough of the bars for the lion to rip the rest apart with his paws.

"RUN FOR YOUR LIVES!" shrieked Chip.

The otters and beavers all fled in different directions. Mama Brown and Mama Black directed the young ones down to the water and the elderly otters ran and hid behind rocks. Papa Black and Papa Brown instinctively resumed their role as zigzagging decoys and tried to draw the mountain lion away from their families.

"This way, you big sack of cat-nip!"

hollered Papa Brown.

"Or are you just a big scaredy-cat?" yelled Papa Black.

But the young lion had learnt his lesson from last time. He ignored the adult otters, even as they stopped and wiggled their bottoms and taunted him by blowing loud raspberries. This time he went for the slowest prey – and that was the beavers!

The Saw Sisters had already dashed into the forest, leaving Twiggy, Chuck and Chip out in the open. The beavers raced around rocks as they tried to get back to the river, but the mountain lion was faster and blocked their path, driving them up the riverbank towards the forest.

Chuck and Twiggy bravely positioned themselves between the big cat and their son, snarling and bearing their teeth, giving Chip time to join his sisters. As he reached the edge of the trees, the young kit turned to see the mountain lion leap into the air and trap his parents' flat tails under his paws.

The otters gasped in horror when the beavers were caught and immediately swam back to shore to help. Papa Brown and Papa Black doubled back too. But no one knew how to save the beavers, and… luckily they didn't need to.

Up in the forest Chip licked his finger and held it up to the wind as Holly, Willow and Hazel did what they do best. The Saw Sisters were not big on conversation, but working together they could gnaw a tree trunk to a pencil-point and send it crashing down in any direction. They just had to wait for their clever little brother to give them the exact coordinates and, as soon as he dropped his arm in the right direction, they pushed against the pine tree.

"TIMBEEEEER!!!" yelled the beaver siblings in unison.

The mountain lion turned, saw the falling tree careering towards him and released the beavers immediately. He then bounded away at speed, eyes bulging and yelping as the pine branches whipped his bottom. The big cat vanished in the canopy as the trunk hit the ground with a boom and a giant cloud of dust filled the air.

"YEEAAAW!" was the last thing the water mammals heard. When the dust cloud cleared, it revealed that the mountain lion was now trapped by *his* tail under the fallen tree.

The young beavers hurried out of the forest and hugged their parents. Then they joined the otters and gathered round the captive cat once more, although this time he was looking more sorry for himself than scary.

"Now, let's try this again, shall we?" said Papa Brown, who approached the mountain lion, but stayed out of reach of those mighty paws. "The same offer still stands."

"And for the record, there are plenty more trees to fell," warned Chuck, standing alongside him.

The otters and the beavers held their collective breath and watched the mountain lion as he assessed his predicament and how to get out of it. After a moment, the beast lowered his massive head and admitted defeat. The otters and beavers exhaled with relief.

The Saw Sisters instantly set to work on the section of tree that was holding down the lion and turned it into a pile of shavings and sawdust in no time. Grandpa Bruno and Grandpa Jack stood by with raised fists, just in case the big cat changed his mind, but the animal upheld his end of the truce and headed back to the forest. He had had quite enough of river mammals and did not intend to return.

The otters and beavers watched the mountain lion slip away unharmed, except for a sore tail tip and wounded pride. They waited until he was out of hearing range before they looked at each other with wide-eyed excitement and took a deep breath.

"HOORAY!" they all cheered together, dancing up and down happily.

Chapter Nine

Friends and Fish!

The beavers and the otters soon set about breaking down the contraptions, sweeping away shells and stones and mopping up fish oil. The Saw Sisters made short work of the fallen tree, turning what remained into a large raft for transporting the rest of the wood upstream, which the young otters sorted into logs, planks and twigs. Beavers recycle everything and could build a whole new wing to their lodge with what they were taking away.

Once everything was done, Chuck and Twiggy made their way down to the water's edge.

"We're off home, then," said Chuck, yawning loudly. Having been up all night constructing the massive lion-trap, the beavers were tired and in need of a good day's sleep.

"Thank you for all your help," said Mama Brown, standing on the mooring pad, along with Mama Black and their

husbands. The otters all smiled and waved goodbye at the beavers as they dived into the water.

"Aren't we going to ask them about the fish again?" whispered Papa Brown through the corner of his mouth, still smiling as the beavers resurfaced by the edge of the raft. "Now that we're being friendly and all, they might take the dam down."

"I'm not sure we can ask them to move upstream any more," whispered Papa Black. "Not now we all appear to like each other."

"They do seem rather nice," said Mama Black, still waving.

"I agree," said Mama Brown. "It would be rude to make new friends and then ask them to go away."

Chip was the last beaver to leave Cottonwood Lodge. He reluctantly headed down to the water, followed by his new best friends, Woody and Sooty.

"Thank you for helping me with my plan," said Chip, still wide awake with excitement. "I couldn't have done it without you both."

"We didn't really do anything," said Woody. "It was all your idea."

"And it worked a treat!" added Sooty.

"Apart from the bit where we almost got eaten!" laughed Chip.

"Your dad seemed pretty proud of you," said Woody.

"I think he realised that thinking and planning can be as important as chopping and building," whispered Chip. "I'll soon find out when I tell him about my new ideas for the dam – they're pretty unusual!"

"Good luck!" said Woody and Sooty together.

Chip swam to catch up with his family, who were pushing the raft upstream towards the dam, while the otters still waved from the riverbank.

Later that afternoon the raft sailed back downstream. The wood was all gone and Chip was standing on the edge, steering the craft with his flat tail, dipping it into

the water like a rudder. He stopped the raft
in the middle of the river and called and
waved to the two otter families that were
lounging around on the mooring pad.

The otters appeared just as exhausted as the beavers had been after working through the night. But instead of suffering from a lack of sleep, they were just hungry. They hadn't eaten anything all day except Mama Black and Mama Brown's Fish Pie Surprise, which was a brand-new recipe. It had an outer crust of crispy riverweed and a filling of riverweed blobs in a riverweed sauce, so the only 'surprise' was that the fish pie contained no fish whatsoever.

"What's he saying?" asked Grandma Maple, squinting at the kit.

"Something about a clam?" asked Beanie, hopefully.

"I think he wants us to see the *dam*,"

suggested Sooty. "He mentioned that he had plans to make some changes to it."

"I bet it's something amazing," said Woody.

"Wasn't the dam big enough already?" grumbled Grandpa Bruno. "Perhaps they're not content with cutting off our fish supply. Maybe they would like to blot out the sun too!"

"Don't be like that," said Mama Brown. "Let's swim upstream and take a look at what they've done." Mama Brown was using a tone of voice saved for occasions when refusal was not an option.

The otters all noted the special tone and dived into the water. Woody and Sooty joined Chip, riding on top of the raft, and noticed that the young beaver seemed very excited.

"I showed my parents the plans for additions to the dam and they thought it was a great idea," he said. "In fact, they liked it so much they put off going to bed and went straight to work after we left you!"

They pushed the raft past the river bend and carried on towards the waiting beavers. The otters all looked at the dam and frowned at each other. It wasn't that they didn't like the changes – they just couldn't work out what was different about it. It appeared to be the same huge heap of logs and branches they'd seen last time.

"Oh, my goodness!" gasped Mama Brown as Chip hopped from the raft and joined his sisters and parents on the dam. "I've never seen anything so beautiful!"

"I agree," said Mama Black. "It really is quite breathtaking!"

"That's very kind of you to say so," Chuck frowned, shifting uncomfortably. "We didn't actually change anything on top, but it's nice to know the classic birds-nest-filled-with-hedgehogs design is still appreciated."

"The changes are all underwater," grinned Twiggy.

The Saw Sisters opened their mouths

to say something, but were too excited to speak. So they hopped up and down instead, clapping their paws together with glee.

"My talented daughters did all the complicated construction and followed their brother's plans beautifully," said Chuck, patting his son on the head. "But it was all Chip's idea, so I think he should be the one to show you."

The otters gathered round, with Sooty and Woody at the front, as Chip lifted a paw and pulled down what looked like an ordinary branch. But it was actually a long lever, similar to those used in the lion trap. There was a loud clunk and then the sound of grinding wheels and cogs, but no one had any idea what they were meant to be looking at.

"Fish!" gasped Beanie, peering into the water. "I just saw a fish!"

"Are you sure it wasn't fish-shaped riverweed?" grumbled Grandpa Bruno.

"I just saw one too!" said Woody, pointing to the left. "I think it was a salmon!"

"And crayfish!" said Sooty, pointing to the right. "There are loads of them!"

The otters watched the colourful fish shapes darting past the raft and dived off to get a closer look. Once underwater, they could see why the beavers were so pleased with their work. Running along the bottom of the dam was a complicated network of cogs and levers that opened and closed wooden flaps. The flaps allowed fish to pass through at the lightest touch and closed again afterwards so the water level on the beavers' side of the dam remained high.

The otters dashed about in the river, chasing the fish and each other, doing somersaults and backflips. They gathered clams and crayfish and anything that wasn't green or riverweedy. Then they all swam back to the surface, with arms and mouths full of food, to thank their neighbours.

But, scanning the length of the dam, they found the beavers were nowhere to be seen.

"Where are they?" asked Sooty.

"I think I hear them," said Woody, and everyone stopped and listened, tilting their heads to a distant noise.

"ZZZZZZ! ZZZZZZ! ZZZZZZ!"

Deep rumbling snores were coming from the entrance to the beavers' lodge, growing louder with every moment that passed. It seemed Chuck, Twiggy, Chip and the Saw Sisters were finally catching up with their sleep.

When the beavers awoke later that evening, after a well-earned rest, they stepped out of their lodge and dived in the water to find that the otters had gone home. Then they spotted the raft with a little pile of crayfish in the middle.

Beavers like a crayfish supper as much as any other river mammal, so they hopped aboard the raft and polished off the pile in no time. Only then did they notice the long rope of knotted riverweed tied to the raft and, when they hauled it in, the raft moved forward, pulling them downstream.

The rope stretched all the way round the river-bend, over the mooring pad of Cottonwood Lodge and down through the entrance. The beavers followed it all the way to the large central chamber and found the otters sitting in front of an enormous fishy banquet, smiling at their baffled guests.

"We were meant to do this earlier," said Mama Brown, standing up and beaming at the sight of their neighbours. "But for one reason or another we were unable."

"I don't understand," said Chuck.

"You tell them, Grandpa," said Woody, as he and Sooty nudged the reluctant old otter out of his seat and, for the first time in a long while, he didn't appear grumpy at all, owing to a belly full of fish.

"We just wanted to invite you all to Cottonwood Lodge for an otter feast, and to say…" said Grandpa Bruno, opening his arms and smiling so everyone could stand and join in together.

"WELCOME TO THE NEIGHBOURHOOD!" cheered the otters.

The beavers didn't need to be asked twice. They sat down and ate heartily with their neighbours, and the otters were happy to share their fishy feast and their small section of the river with their new friends.

Epilogue

High above the river in the Wild West forest, the mountain lion paced along the tree-line at the edge of the riverbank, considering his options, as the water mammals celebrated their new-found friendship.

The lion planned to honour his promise to steer clear of the otters and beavers, but he was worried what might happen if he encountered one of them by accident. He gazed up at the tall, heavy pine trees and tucked his tail underneath him with a shudder. Perhaps the safest thing would be to move far away from the river altogether.

So the mountain lion turned back into the forest and crossed the stream and kept on going. He walked for days and days into the *wild* Wild West, which was so far from the river that no otters or beavers were ever likely to bother him.

But, like the beavers with the otters, he soon discovered that his new home was

already spoken for. The mountain lion had
entered another animal's territory, and he
was about to begin a brand-new friendship
of his own with a mountain lioness.

Find out how the Brown family and the Black family met in the first OTTER CHAOS adventure!

Woddy the otter pup is splish-splash happy! His family are moving to a big new den downstream. But when they arrive, another family are already there! The only way to decide who stays is an otterly chaotic sports day! On your marks get set... GO!

Awesome Animals

Awesome adventures with the **wildest** wildlife!